Grandfather's
Dance

PATRICIA MacLACHLAN

Grandfather's Dance

JOANNA COTLER BOOKS

HarperTrophy®

An Imprint of HarperCollins*Publishers*

Harper Trophy® is a registered trademark of HarperCollins Publishers.

Grandfather's Dance
Copyright © 2006 by Patricia MacLachlan

Library of Congress Cataloging-in-Publication Data
MacLachlan, Patricia.
Grandfather's dance / by Patricia MacLachlan. — 1st ed.
p.   cm.
Summary: As her family gathers for the wedding of her sister Anna, fourth-grader
Cassie Witting sees the many changes brought about by everyday life and finds comfort
in the love of those around her, especially her grandfather.
ISBN 978-0-06-134003-1
[1. Family life—Fiction. 2. Grandfathers—Fiction.] I. Title.
PZ7.M2225Gr 2006   2006000463
[Fic]—dc22   CIP
                                                                                     AC

Typography by Neil Swaab
❖
First Harper Trophy edition, 2008

For my husband, Bob—
always my first reader

And for my father, Philo (1902–2004)—
who danced
—P.M.

His name is John, my little brother. John Jacob Witting, after my papa and grandfather. But Papa and Mama call him Jack. Jack calls himself Doggie. He calls a lot of people Doggie.

"Doggie wants milk," he says at the dinner table.

When Mama ignores him, he says, "Please . . . Doggie says please."

He can run now, so Mama has to chase after him.

Around the house . . .

Out to the barn . . .

And into the meadow . . .

He's so little that he can get lost in the fields of corn.

Every day I hurry home from school to see him. I never expected to like him. Or to love him.

"I will never love this horrible new baby," I told my sister, Anna. "I won't speak to the baby ever, either."

But I was wrong.

Maybe I am under a spell like in a fairy tale. Maybe someone somewhere has cursed me.

I can't help it.

I love him.

1

Spring. School was hard in the spring. Even fourth grade was hard. The windows of the small school were open and the sweet smell of new grass blew in. I couldn't pay attention. Neither could Ian or Min or Grace. Will was half asleep, and Isabel looked out the window. There were only six of us in school, from first grade to fifth. Mr. Willet read out loud to us, but no one seemed to hear. One of the horses whinnied outside and we all looked out the window. Finally Mr. Willet put down his book and looked out the window, too.

"Let's go home," he said softly.

Ian, the youngest of everyone, only six, clapped his hands, making Mr. Willet laugh.

"Go home, go on home," he said, still laughing. "We'll try again on Monday."

I gathered my books and helped Ian with his. I made sure he got home every day. Today I'd ridden Molly, and I gave Ian a leg up. We rode together, Ian's arms around my waist.

"Caleb and I used to ride home from school just like this," I said.

"Caleb's big now," said Ian.

"Yes. He's big. Away at school."

"Do you miss him?"

"Yes. I miss Caleb."

"Does he tease you?" asked Ian.

"Yes, Caleb has always teased me."

"I tease my little sister every single day," said Ian.

I heard him yawn behind me, and I turned and wrapped a long scarf behind him and tied it in front of my waist. Sometimes Ian fell asleep on the way home. I didn't want him falling off Molly.

"Lily loves me even if I tease her," said Ian matter-of-factly.

"Yes."

"Let's do twosies," said Ian.

"Okay. Two times two is . . . ?"

"Four."

"Two times three is . . . ?"

"Six."

Ian laid his head against my back and Molly walked slowly down the road to his house.

"Two times four?"

Ian didn't answer. I smiled. He'd fallen asleep, his breath warm on my back.

Way off in the fields, meadowlarks flew and the smell of prairie spring followed us home.

———◆———

"Cassie! Cassie!"

Jack ran out of the barn, Papa and our dog Lottie following him. His pale hair was long and curly around his face. Mama once said he looked like an angel. Grandfather said most times he didn't act like one.

The surprise was that Jack did act like an angel around Grandfather. He never frowned at Grandfather. He never showed Grandfather his temper. Every evening he sat on Grandfather's lap and made him tell a story, made him sing. From the very beginning, Grandfather had been Jack's favorite.

Papa lifted Jack up to sit with me on Molly. Jack leaned down and kissed Molly on her neck, and we went into the barn.

"Doggie," said Jack.

I smiled.

"Horse," I said to him. "Molly's a horse."

Jack turned and frowned his fierce frown at me.

"Doggie," said Jack, making me laugh.

I kissed the top of his head. It was warm and sweet smelling.

"All right," I said. "Doggie."

"Horse," said Jack, smiling back at me.

"A joke!" I cried. "You made a joke, Jack."

I got off Molly and reached up and slid Jack down beside me.

"Doggie," whispered Jack.

I laughed and took his hand. We walked out of the cool, dark barn into the light. He jumped up and down beside me as we walked.

His hand was tiny and warm in my hand.

2

We ate stew for dinner—Grandfather, Mama, Papa, Jack and I, Jack in his wooden high chair.

"You came home early today, Cassie," Mama said.

I nodded.

"Spring came in the window," I said.

"Now, there's a poem," said Mama, smiling at me.

"Mr. Willet said that he couldn't pay attention, either. So we all came home."

"And Ian?" asked Mama.

"Fell asleep in the middle of twosies," I said.

"There's a poem again," said Grandfather.

"Doggie wants stew, please," said Jack.

Everyone laughed.

"That's a nice 'please,' little Doggie," said Papa, spooning some stew into Jack's bowl.

Papa took a letter out of his jacket pocket.

"I forgot, Sarah. This came today from your brother."

Mama grinned.

"The aunts and William! I invited them to Anna's wedding."

Quickly, Mama opened the letter.

"Old women in the house. That's all we need," grumped Grandfather.

"That from an old man, of course," said Papa.

"They're coming! All of them!" said Mama. "Except for Meg. Meg can't come."

Meg was William's wife.

Mama's eyes filled with tears.

Papa got up and put his arms around her.

"I know," he said softly. "It's been a long, long time."

"Where will they stay?" I asked.

"In the barn," whispered Grandfather. "We'll throw down some blankets."

"We'll make room," said Papa. "Harriet and Mattie and Lou can stay in Caleb's room. *That's* something to think about."

"*I'll* stay in the barn," said Grandfather in a strong voice.

"Doggie stay in barn," said Jack.

Grandfather reached over and took Jack's hand.

"You bet," he said.

———◆———

It was dark outside. Mama was sewing, the light of the lamp falling across a white dress. The dogs sat nearby, Lottie at her feet, Nick by the wood stove.

"What are you doing?"

Mama looked up.

"I'm sewing my old wedding dress. For Anna."

I nodded.

"Why do people get married?" I asked.

"They love each other. They want to spend their lives together."

"I don't love anyone for marrying," I said. "Except for Lottie and Nick. Do you think I could marry a dog?"

Mama smiled.

"That would be nice," she said. "They are always glad to see you. Always forgiving if you speak sharply to them. They love you no matter what."

She bit off a piece of thread.

"I think marrying a dog would be splendid."

"Me, too."

Mama and I smiled at each other.

"You're happy that the aunts are coming?"

"And my brother, William."

"I don't remember him," I said.

Mama shook her head.

"You weren't born, Cassie. But you'll like him, Cass. He's wonderful." She stood and

held up the white satin dress. "Wonderful."
She looked at me and grinned.

"Like a dog."

---

*It is my wedding, and I am in my long
white dress. There are many, many people
there. The sun is overhead and a breeze
blows my veil. I am beautiful.*

*Everyone turns to watch Papa walk
me down through the garden. Everyone
smiles. Mama is there, and Jack, who is
quite tall. And Caleb, home from school.
And Anna. I can't see Grandfather.
Where is he?*

*At the end of our walk is my wonderful,
tall husband-to-be. He is black and white,
with a long feathered tail. He wags it. He is
beautiful. We will live happily ever after.*

It bothered me that Grandfather was not at my wedding.

"Where were you?" I asked him when I read my journal to him.

Grandfather looked a little sad, but he smiled.

"I was in the barn," he whispered.

3

The days grew warmer and now it was light long into the evening. Mama and Papa and Anna planned the wedding. Anna had come from her room in town with pictures and lists.

And Jack began to talk and act like Grandfather. He called Grandfather "Boppa," his own private name for Grandfather. He tried to walk like him, with his hands behind his back. Once Anna and I saw them both walking to the barn this way, Jack just behind Grandfather.

"Peas in a pod," said Anna.

Jack began to say everything Grandfather said.

"Yep," said Grandfather.

"Yep," said Jack.

"You bet."

"You bet!"

When Grandfather slept on the daybed, Jack lay down beside him, watching him closely. Jack lay back with his hands across his chest and tried to snore.

Papa came in from the barn and smiled at them.

"Jack is a very small Grandfather," I said to Papa.

"He sounds like John more and more every day," Mama said. "Pretty soon he'll start being stubborn and cranky."

And he did.

Anna and Justin came to dinner. They would be married soon, and there was talk of flowers and food and music.

"Eat your beans, Jack," said Mama, pointing to his plate.

"Doggie no beans," said Jack, frowning.

"They're good, Jack," said Justin.

"No," said Jack.

Grandfather dropped his fork on the floor.

"Drat," he said.

"I'd like you to eat some beans, Jack," repeated Mama.

Jack climbed down out of his chair.

"Drat, drat, drat," he yelled.

Everyone was quiet.

Grandfather finally spoke.

"That sounded . . . a little bit . . . like . . ."

"You, Boppa," said Papa.

Grandfather sighed and stood up.

"I guess I'm the one who should take care of this," he said.

He took Jack's hand and they went outside.

Mama bit her lip. Papa stared at his plate. Suddenly, Mama began to laugh. We laughed, too.

"Poor John," said Mama. "This is a very hard job. Keeping Jack in line behind him."

"Huge," said Anna.

"Nearly impossible," said Justin.

And they began to laugh all over again.

A long time later, Grandfather and Jack came back. They were very quiet. They sat next to each other at the table where Mama and Papa and Anna and Justin were drinking coffee.

Grandfather poked Jack gently.

Jack looked up at Grandfather.

"Doggie sorry," said Jack.

Grandfather poked Jack again.

"Jack sorry," said Jack, using his name for the first time.

Grandfather sat back.

"That's very good," he said, pleased with himself.

"Drat," whispered Jack.

———•———

The aunts were coming by train. In seven days. Mama's brother, William, would come after.

"Two weeks of aunts," said Papa. "That's a lot of aunts."

"They'll help," said Mama.

"Oh, I know that," said Papa, laughing. "They may take over."

"I remember the aunts," said Anna. "Papa made all of us leave here when the land dried up."

"He stayed here all alone, while we were in beautiful green Maine with the aunts," said Mama. "By the ocean that stretched out like the prairie. Where it rained all the time, while Papa waited and waited for rain."

"How far does the ocean stretch out?" I asked.

"As far as you can see."

"Just like the prairie here," I said.

"Just like here," said Anna, smiling.

"Then, when it finally rained, Papa came to surprise us. And the aunts loved him."

"And I loved the aunts, too," said Papa.

"And then we came home," said Anna.

"And I was born," I said.

"You were."

Anna put on the wedding veil that Mama had pressed. She looked at herself in the mirror.

"You look beautiful," said Mama.

Anna turned.

"I remember when you wore this, Sarah."

Mama smiled. "You were a little girl when I married your papa. And now look at you."

"Maybe I'll wear the dress and veil when I marry my dog," I said.

Anna laughed and put the veil on my head.

I stared at myself in the mirror. Anna saw my look.

"There is something about a veil, Cassie. It is like a spell cast over you. It makes you beautiful no matter how young or old or plain you think you are."

My husband dog licks my cheek and whispers, "You have never been more beautiful. You're more beautiful than a pot roast."

We washed the floors in Caleb's and Anna's rooms. We moved three beds into Caleb's bedroom for the aunts. We straightened and dusted and painted a table and bookcase blue.

"Blue looks nice in this room," I said.

"All this trouble for old girls," said Grandfather.

"You'd better be careful," warned Papa. "Your small friend repeats everything."

Grandfather straightened and looked around, alarmed.

"I have to watch myself all the time," he muttered.

"He loves you," said Papa.

"Well, I've had just about enough of his love," Grandfather complained.

Then he looked at Papa.

"That's not so."

"I know," said Papa.

4

A surprise. Papa had gone off to town early on Zeke, the dapple-gray horse. Mama and I were baking bread when we heard the sound of a motor outside. Mama looked out the window.

"Oh my," she said. "Oh my!"

She ran out, leaving the door open behind her. I took Jack's hand and we followed her. Grandfather was coming out of the barn. He stopped suddenly and stared.

Zeke was tied to the back of a car. Papa untied him and took him to the paddock.

"A car! It's beautiful, Jacob," said Mama.

The car was a shiny dark gray with silver trim. It had soft seats.

Mama smiled. "You did this for the wedding, didn't you?"

Papa nodded. "And for the aunts," he said.

He looked proud, but when Papa talked about it he sounded like Grandfather.

"It may be beautiful," he grumped, "but I'll take Zeke any day. Zeke eats and takes me places and waits. He's an old friend. He's loyal. I don't see anything loyal about this car. It doesn't love me."

Grandfather peered in the windows.

"Maybe it doesn't matter," he said.

Grandfather opened a door and got inside. He put his hands on the wheel for a moment, then rolled down the window.

"Maybe something so beautiful doesn't have to be loyal," he said to Papa.

Papa folded back the engine cover and looked inside. He shook his head.

"Too many parts," he said. "Zeke's beautiful. And loyal. Aren't you, Zeke?" he called.

At the sound of his name, Zeke looked

over his shoulder at Papa. Then he went back to eating grass.

"And Zeke loves me," said Papa. "This car doesn't love me."

"Zeke," whispered Jack.

———•———

We rode to town the next day. Grandfather had to see Dr. Sam, Justin's father. We would buy food and supplies for the aunts.

Grandfather sat in front, next to Papa, because his legs were too long for the back-seat. Mama and Jack and I sat in back, Jack on my lap, looking out the window.

"Bye-bye, Zeke," called Jack, making Grandfather laugh.

"The aunts will love this, Jacob," said Mama. "You can pick them up at the train in style."

"Better than three old women on a dapple-gray horse," said Grandfather.

Papa looked back over his shoulder at

Jack, who sat quietly, looking at the prairie pass by.

"Zeke could handle it," he said softly to Grandfather.

"Not sure the aunts could," whispered Grandfather.

It was quiet in the car, except for the motor running. There was no sound of big wagon wheels turning, or wind whipping around our heads, or rain soaking us if it rained. Or worse, snow in winter. It was so quiet that Jack fell asleep long before we crossed over the railroad tracks and got into town.

There were horses and wagons and cars in town. Papa parked the car in front of Dr. Sam's office.

Grandfather opened the door.

"We'll meet you at the store when you're ready," said Mama.

Anna worked for Dr. Sam. Her eyes widened when she came out of the office and saw the car.

Papa laughed.

Anna hugged Grandfather and peered into the car.

"How does Zeke feel about this?" she asked Papa.

"He's on a little holiday," said Papa.

"For the aunts," said Jack, his thin voice startling everyone. And then he added what Papa was afraid he would. In a clear voice, so easy to hear, like a little bell in the wind.

"Three old women on a dapple-gray horse."

———•———

That night Grandfather had to move into Jack's bedroom to make room for all the people who would come to the wedding: the aunts, William, and Caleb—who would be home from school. Jack was very happy. He sat on his bed and watched Mama and Papa move Grandfather's bed in.

I carried in some shirts to Grandfather.

"This is not forever," Grandfather said to Jack. "You understand?"

Jack smiled at Grandfather.

"This is my bed, pal. And that is yours," said Grandfather, pointing.

"Pal," said Jack happily.

"All moved in?" asked Mama at the door.

Jack looked up.

"Pal!" he repeated.

"Thank you for this, John," Mama said to Grandfather. "I know this isn't the way you'd want it to be. You look tired. Are you all right?"

"Old," said Grandfather, sitting down. "Older every day."

He took some pills out of his pocket. I knew he had gotten more pills from Dr. Sam.

"Well, I thank you, John."

"You bet, Sarah," he said.

"You bet, Sarah," Jack said.

———•◆•———

"Do you have a story today?" asked Ian.

Ian and I rode home. It was the last day of school. We had packed up our notebooks and said good-bye to Mr. Willet. The day was warm. Summer was here.

"Do you?" he repeated. "Have a story?"

"I'm out of stories," I said. "My head is busy, Ian. The aunts are coming tomorrow. The wedding is a week after."

Grandfather's getting older. Older every day.

"A happy story about a wedding would make me sleepy," said Ian. "A hero's wedding."

Ian could always make me smile.

Prairie dogs scampered alongside the road.

"Once there was a strong and brave prairie dog," I said.

Ian laughed.

"What was his name?"

"Monty."

"How brave was he?" asked Ian.

He laid his head on my back, and I hoped he'd fall asleep soon so I wouldn't have to make up a long story.

"He could fly as high as the clouds. He saved lost cattle and put out fires. And once he tied up a robber."

"What was the robber's name?"

"Ian," I said. And Ian laughed again.

"Was he nice?"

"Oh, yes, he was kind and good. They gave him a huge wedding party in town, and all his prairie dog friends came. There was dancing."

"Who did he marry?"

"The Princess Prairie Dog."

"Was it a happy wedding?" asked Ian, yawning.

"Yes. It was the best wedding in the world."

I reached down to pat Molly's neck. It was warm from the sun.

"The end," I said.

Molly walked on. Ian didn't ask any more

questions. Just as he had said he would, he had fallen asleep.

———•◆•———

That night, when I woke in the middle of the night and went downstairs to get a drink of water, I looked in Jack's bedroom. In Grandfather's bed was Jack, curled up like a small cat under Grandfather's chin. Lottie and Nick slept on Jack's bed.

5

The aunts wore hats.

The car drove into the yard in the late afternoon, and the aunts got out, wearing dresses with lace trim, and stockings and hats.

Even Aunt Lou, who Caleb told me usually wore overalls and worked with animals. She walked over to the paddock fence. Zeke and Bess and Molly came over right away so she could rub their noses. Two of the sheep came, too.

Grandfather and I watched through the upstairs window as Mama and Jack went out for hugs and kisses.

"The ship of aunts has arrived," said Grandfather softly. "Aren't you going down?"

I nodded.

"You'll be nice, won't you?" I said to him.

"I will be as charming as a prince," said Grandfather.

"We'll see," I said.

I left Grandfather laughing behind me. I went out to hug Aunt Harriet and Aunt Mattie and Aunt Lou.

———•———

Aunt Harriet surprised Grandfather right away. She brought her flute, which did not impress Grandfather.

"You don't have to like it," she told Grandfather when she saw the look on his face. "I didn't bring it for you."

She also brought a deck of cards and invited him to play. They played many games, and Aunt Harriet beat Grandfather every time. While Aunt Mattie helped Mama with her dress for the wedding, Aunt Harriet kept winning into the night. Lamplight fell across the cards on the table long after Jack had gone to bed.

"I'm not amused," said Grandfather as Aunt Harriet won again.

"That's all right. I am," she said.

"Me, too," I told her.

———◆———

Aunt Lou was up early, dressed in overalls. She and Papa sat at the table drinking coffee and having a peppy discussion. Jack sat between them, his head turning from one side to the other as they talked. I stood in the doorway, listening.

"Why?" asked Papa.

"I want to," said Aunt Lou.

"Do you have a permit to drive?" asked Papa.

"Yes," said Aunt Lou quickly.

Papa smiled slightly.

Jack smiled, too.

"Well . . . where is it?" asked Papa.

Aunt Lou took a deep breath and went to find her bag.

"Good morning, Cassie," said Papa.

"Good morning," I said, coming into the kitchen. Grandfather came after me, pouring coffee and sitting next to Jack.

"Pal!" said Jack.

"Pal," said Grandfather, putting his hand over Jack's hand.

Aunt Lou handed Papa a folded piece of paper.

"Here."

Papa looked at it, then at Aunt Lou.

"This says *Lou can drive*, signed, *Horace Bricker*."

Aunt Lou nodded.

"Yes, Horace taught me how to drive. That's proof."

Papa's mouth opened. He looked at me, then closed it again.

"How about," said Papa slowly, handing the paper back to Aunt Lou, "you drive on the tractor roads that go through the meadows. Could you do that?"

"Oh yes!" said Aunt Lou happily. "You

didn't think I wanted to drive on the main roads, did you? With all the fools out there?"

She tapped Grandfather on the shoulder.

"How about it, John? Want to go driving? Past the slough and across the far meadows? We can go fast!"

She stopped and looked at Papa.

"We *can* go fast, can't we?"

Papa put his hands over his eyes and leaned on the table.

Jack put his hands over his eyes and leaned on the table, too.

We speed across the prairie, birds scattering, prairie dogs disappearing down their holes. Grandfather sits in the front seat next to Aunt Lou. He laughs. I sit in the back.

The slough whizzes by.

Zeke and three cows lift their heads and watch us pass.

Sheep scatter.

Grandfather and Aunt Lou laugh. We drive up a hill and all I can see is the blue sky above and around us.

I hang on to a handle in front of me. I'm scared.

And then, after a moment, I begin to laugh, too.

Mama, Papa, Jack, Aunt Mattie, and Aunt Harriet had gone to bed.

Aunt Lou and Grandfather drank tea at the kitchen table.

"That was very fast," I said. "I've never gone that fast on the prairie. Except maybe galloping on a horse."

Aunt Lou smiled at me over her cup.

"If I'd been writing in my journal, my

dog husband would have chased the car," I said. "I almost looked out the back window to see if he was there."

Aunt Lou put down her cup.

"If he'd been chasing the car, I would have stopped for him," she said.

"Thank you," I said.

She looked at Grandfather.

"And how did you like the ride?" she asked.

"You're a madwoman," he said.

Aunt Lou smiled.

"I live life to the brim," she said.

"And a little over the top, I'd say," said Grandfather.

6

The next day Jack got sick. At supper he came into the kitchen, holding Aunt Mattie's hand, his blanket trailing behind him. He climbed up on Grandfather's lap.

"You want some soup, pal?" asked Grandfather. "Aunt Mattie made it."

Jack shook his head and leaned back against Grandfather.

"He feels warm, Sarah," said Aunt Mattie.

Mama leaned over and put her lips on Jack's forehead.

"Oh, Jack. You *are* warm."

She picked him up and sat him on her lap. Jack buried his head in her shoulder.

"He has a fever," she said. "Cassie, would you get some juice, please?"

"Not a good time for him to be sick, is it? The wedding and all," said Papa.

"There's never a good time," said Mama.

I poured orange juice and handed it to Jack. He shook his head.

"Come on, Jack," said Grandfather, picking him up. "We'll rock in the chair. We could, in fact, rock all through the wedding. They don't need us."

"Sing," said Jack.

"I was waiting for that," said Papa, grinning.

Grandfather sighed.

"Sing," Jack said again.

"*Twinkle, twinkle, little star . . .*" began Grandfather. "*How I wonder . . .*"

Jack shook his head.

"No?" said Grandfather.

He began again.

"*Hush, little baby, don't say a word. Papa's*

going to buy you a mockingbird. And if that mockingbird don't sing . . ."

Jack put his hand over Grandfather's mouth.

The aunts laughed.

"I know the one he wants," I said.

Grandfather didn't say anything for a moment. Papa looked up. He knew, too. Grandfather had sung the song to him when he was little. Then Grandfather began his song. Jack didn't stop him. He lay back and closed his eyes as Grandfather's soft voice filled the kitchen. The aunts were very quiet. Aunt Mattie put down her knitting and listened. The dogs looked up.

> *"Sleep, my love, and peace attend thee,*
> *All through the night;*
> *Guardian angels God will lend thee,*
> *All through the night.*
> *Soft the drowsy hours are creeping.*
> *Hill and dale in slumber steeping,*

I my loving vigil keeping,
All through the night."

It was very quiet. And then there was a
rustle at the door.

"You sang that song when you first
came, Grandfather," said Caleb. "When
Cassie found you. A long time ago."

We all turned.

"Caleb!" I cried.

Caleb put his finger to his lips so Jack
wouldn't wake. I hugged him. Mama did,
too. And Papa.

"How did you get here?" asked Mama.

Caleb smiled as the door opened.

"Dr. Sam gave me a ride," said Caleb.

"I had to come," said Dr. Sam. "To have
a look at the aunts."

Grandfather laughed.

"Well, this is Harriet, and Mattie, and
Lou," said Caleb, touching each one on the
shoulder.

"How do you do? Didn't you have sheep

by those names?" Dr. Sam asked Mama.

Mama smiled.

"Yes, I saw Mattie the sheep just yesterday," said Aunt Lou. "She's a bit fat."

"Sam, could you have a look at Jack?" said Mama. "He's got a fever."

Dr. Sam put his hand on Jack's forehead. Jack didn't wake.

"He's warm, for sure. Could be the beginnings of a cold. Make sure he has lots of water," said Dr. Sam.

He took his stethoscope out of his pocket and listened to Jack's chest.

"A little congested. Keep an eye on him. Call me if you need me."

He smiled at Mama.

"Wedding is four days away. Are you ready?"

"I am. I've been ready for Anna to marry your son for a long time."

"We'll be family," said Dr. Sam.

Papa said what we all knew.

"You've always been family," he said.

It was quiet. Then, all of a sudden, there was Jack's clear voice.

"Caleb's home!" he said, making us all smile.

———•◆•———

Dr. Sam felt Grandfather's forehead before he left.

"And how are you?"

"Tired," said Grandfather.

"You might catch what Jack has," warned Dr. Sam.

"Maybe," said Grandfather. "Maybe I'm too old."

"That's a nice car you have," said Aunt Lou, looking out the window.

"Would you like a ride?" asked Dr. Sam.

"I would," said Aunt Lou.

"Don't, under any circumstances, let her drive," Grandfather whispered to Dr. Sam.

———•◆•———

That night Aunt Mattie gave me a box wrapped in bright paper.

"What is it?" I asked.

"Open it," she said. "I made it for you. There's so much fuss for Anna that I was afraid you'd get lost."

Caleb put his arm around me.

"Cassie? Cassie's never lost. Except maybe in her head," he said.

In the box was a blue dress made of silk, with a lace top. It had satin ribbons braided in the lace. They flowed down across the dress.

It was so beautiful I could only whisper.

"I've never had a dress so fine," I said softly.

I threw my arms around Aunt Mattie.

"Thank you so much!"

"You will look beautiful," said Aunt Mattie. "We will all look beautiful."

"I plan to," said Aunt Harriet.

"Me, too," said Aunt Lou.

"I plan to attend the wedding in my

underwear," said Grandfather.

Jack raised his head.

"Boppa's underwear," he said.

———•———

When I wrote in my journal it was very late. Everyone had gone to bed except for Caleb and me.

My blue silk wedding dress flows out behind me as my dog husband and I ride Zeke across the prairie: past the sheep, Harriet and Mattie and Lou; past the slough; and past the stand of Russian olive. My ribbons fly out behind me so far that when I look back, I cannot see where they end. Like the prairie.

"Do you like school?" I whispered to Caleb in the upstairs hallway.

"I love it," he said. "But I miss you, Cassie."

We heard Grandfather's voice then, so soft in the dark, singing to Jack.

"Remember that?" asked Caleb.

I nodded, thinking about the time so long ago when I found Grandfather behind the barn. He had come to see his old farm. And he had sung that song.

"Some things don't change," Caleb said softly. "Some things."

Angels watching ever round thee,
All through the night;
In my slumbers close surround thee,
All through the night.

7

The aunts began to cook for the wedding. The kitchen was filled with bowls and platters and pans. Anna came home to help, bringing more plates and silverware. Mama and Caleb and I weeded the gardens and clipped the grasses around the porch. Matthew and Maggie, Mama and Papa's very best friends, brought chairs and tables. Their children, Rose and Violet, came too—Rose to help and Violet to see Caleb. They whispered to each other by the barn, Zeke coming over to nose them.

"Zinnias," said Maggie. "You always loved zinnias."

"You brought them to me when I first came here," Mama said.

"Now it's the first wedding of any of our children," said Maggie happily. "Anna and Justin have known each other for a long time."

"So have they," said Mama with a smile, looking at Violet and Caleb.

"Ah, the young ones," said Maggie.

"Too young," said Matthew briskly.

Maggie and Mama laughed.

"We'll see," said Maggie. "We'll see."

Matthew shook his head. Then everyone straightened, shading their eyes as Papa's car came up the road, sending up little dust clouds behind it.

I looked quickly at Mama. This was what she had been waiting for.

Mama started running as the car turned into the yard. Papa came to a stop and William bounded out of it, lifting Mama up in his arms. William was taller than Mama, but his hair was fair like hers. His face was brown from the sun. William was out at sea every day and fished all day long. His teeth looked very white as he grinned at Mama.

"I miss you!" cried Mama.

"I miss you, too!" said William, his arm around Mama as they walked to the house.

"I miss Meg, too," said Mama.

"So do I!" said William, and they both laughed.

"How was the train?" asked Mama.

"On time! I am impressed."

Mama introduced William to Matthew and Maggie and the girls. Caleb hugged William.

"You're tall," said William.

"I'll catch up with you one day," said Caleb.

Grandfather shook William's hand. Jack hid behind Grandfather shyly.

"I see you, Jack," said William, making Jack smile.

William stopped in front of me.

"Cassie," he said softly.

"How do you know?" I asked.

"You must be Cassie. You look just like

your mama did when she was your age."

"Really?"

"Really. She even had braids like you."

William reached out and touched my hair.

"Did you tease her?" I asked.

"Of course," said William. "It was my job."

The aunts came out of the house then, flour up to their elbows.

"Ah, the cooks!" said William.

"William's here! Now we can have the wedding," announced Aunt Harriet.

———◆———

Jack was content to listen to Grandfather's songs while he was sick. He was happy to sleep next to Grandfather at night. He loved to watch Grandfather eat. The evening William came, Jack asked for coffee with his dessert after supper.

Mama laughed.

"No coffee for you, Jack. That is for grown-ups."

Jack frowned at Mama.

"Coffee?" Jack said to William.

William smiled.

"Coffee?" he asked Grandfather.

Grandfather shook his head.

"No coffee, pal," he said.

Jack fell off his chair onto the floor, crying.

"I'd say Jack's unhappy," said Aunt Mattie with a half smile.

"Coffee won't make him any happier," said Grandfather.

That made Jack cry louder. He kicked his feet against the wood floor. Lottie and Nick came over to sniff him, then moved away to safety.

"Oh, Jack," said Mama. "Come. I'll read you a story."

Jack cried.

"Let's go paint a picture, Jack," said Aunt Lou. "You can use my paint box."

Jack cried louder.

Grandfather got up quickly, so quickly

that his chair fell over backward.

"Jack!" he shouted, his voice louder than I had ever heard it. "Stop that right now."

Jack stopped and stared at Grandfather. We all stared. I had never heard Grandfather lose his temper. I had seen Jack lose his temper many times. He was a little boy. But not Grandfather.

Silence filled the room. Grandfather walked out the kitchen door, slamming it behind him. Jack got up and walked to the window to look out. Caleb and I looked out, too. Outside, moonlight touched the grass and spilled over the flowers in Mama's garden. Grandfather walked toward the barn. Then, suddenly, he stopped, lifted his shoulders, and turned around as if he knew Jack was at the window. And there, in the moonlight, Grandfather did a little dance, turning around and around, his hands in the air.

Jack smiled. Grandfather smiled back at him.

"That's the best apology I've ever seen," said Caleb softly.

"I'll say," said Mama. "Grandfather's sorry, Jack."

"Dance," said Jack. He put his thumb in his mouth, then took it out. "Sorry," he said, so softly that it was almost a whisper.

8

The day before the wedding was sunny and warm. Matthew and Papa put up tents. William and Grandfather built a wooden arch for Justin and Anna to stand under when they married. Tomorrow morning Mama and the aunts would wind in flowers—roses from the bushes by the paddock, zinnias and feverfew. Tomorrow Caleb and I would toss rose petals on the path between the gardens where Anna would walk.

Aunt Lou sat on the porch, rocking Jack. Grandfather walked off a bit and turned to look at the gardens and arch and tents. He put his hands in his pockets. Then he walked slowly to the barn. I followed him.

Inside the barn was cool and dark with the sweet smell of hay and animals. Some chickens had found their way out of the sun into the shade, and pecked here and there.

"What are you doing?" I asked.

Grandfather smiled.

"Thinking," he said. "Thinking about weddings."

"*All* weddings? Or *the* wedding?" I asked.

Grandfather cocked his head to one side, like Nick and Lottie did when they were listening.

"Actually," he said softly, "I was thinking about *your* wedding."

I nodded.

"I may not be able to be at your wedding, Cassie," said Grandfather.

My heart raced. I knew what Grandfather meant.

"You will, Grandfather. Yes, you will!" I could feel my voice rising.

"Maybe," said Grandfather.

He shrugged.

"But just in case I can't be there, I think we should have a wedding."

"You mean tomorrow?"

Grandfather shook his head.

"Now," he whispered. "Get Nick. Go put on your blue dress."

"My dress?"

"Run. Do it now!" said Grandfather.

I grinned. I ran out of the barn and into the sunlight.

"I'm coming to your wedding!" called Grandfather behind me.

It is a fine wedding, my dog husband's and mine.

I wear my blue silk dress with the trailing ribbons. And a veil.

I carry a rose surrounded by feverfew. My dog husband, Nick (whose full

name is Nicholas Wheaton Witting),
wears a zinnia in his collar. He stands
under the arch, looking beautiful and bored.

When I walk the path between the gardens everyone is there, Mama and Papa,
the aunts, Caleb and Jack. Aunt Harriet
plays the flute—

But the best thing of all is that
Grandfather is there waiting for me, smiling.

He gives my dog husband a bone.

"Be good to Cassie," he says.

"Oui," says Nick.

I am astonished. I have never heard
Nick speak French words.

"You speak French!" I cry.

"I retrieve, too," says my dog husband.

"Thank you," I said to Grandfather at
dinner.

"Thank *you*," said Grandfather.

"I feel better," I said.

"I do, too," said Grandfather. He took my hand. "I do, too."

"Well, I am waiting for Nick to speak French," said Mama.

"That *is* impressive," said William.

"He can only speak French in my journal," I said.

"I suppose that's what writing is for," said Grandfather. "To change life and make it come out the way you want it to."

"Speak, Nick. Speak!" said Papa.

Nick cocked his head from one side to the other. He was silent.

"Woof," said Jack finally.

9

Anna and Justin's wedding was almost as fine as my wedding. The sun was overhead when they married. Anna looked like a cloud of silk and tulle. Papa cried.

Grandfather and Jack wore red bow ties and blue shirts, and the aunts were beautiful in flowered dresses and hats. Later they danced.

Matthew and Maggie were there, and Rose and Violet. All of my friends from school were there, laughing and chasing each other, and stealing candied roses off the wedding cake. Mr. Willet, my teacher, was there, too, pretending he didn't see them do it.

The dogs came, blue ribbons tied on

their collars, and our cat Seal's kittens, now grown, wound in and around plants in the garden, watching curiously.

Mama and Papa danced and smiled at each other as if it were their wedding.

William danced with Aunt Mattie and Aunt Lou, one after the other. Grandfather danced with Aunt Harriet once. He looked over her head, out at the prairie. I had never seen him dance before. Except the one time, after he yelled at Jack—his little dance in the moonlight.

Later, after the dancing and food and cake, we threw rose petals and waved good-bye as Anna and Justin went off in Justin's car, a spray of white roses on the back. And then it was quiet. The aunts took off their shoes and fanned themselves and drank lemonade.

"I almost got married once," said Aunt Harriet wistfully.

"Me, too," said Aunt Mattie.

"Not me," said Aunt Lou. "*I* got a dog."

"As did Cassie," said Grandfather.

Grandfather sat on a bench next to the aunts.

"So she did," said Aunt Lou.

"Doggie," said Jack, climbing up on Grandfather's lap. He lay back against Grandfather's shoulder and reached up with his hand to touch Grandfather's cheek. I sat next to Grandfather and he put his arm around me. White clouds hung high in the sky. Birds sang in the meadow.

The world smelled of roses.

———◆———

Papa left the tents up so it was like the end of the wedding for days. There were still vases of flowers on the tables and tablecloths that reached the ground. We ate our lunches and suppers under the white tents, and talked long into the night by candlelight. Lottie and Nick slept under the tablecloths, hidden and cool. Caleb stayed, and it was like before, when

Caleb was home, teasing me every day.

Aunt Harriet played music in the evening sometimes. Grandfather learned to like the sound of her flute. Once he sang as she played:

"Sumer is icumen in
Lhude sing cuccu!"

His voice was strong and sweet at the same time.

"I learned that song from Sarah," he told the aunts.

"And she learned it from us," they told him.

In the evenings we laughed. Grandfather told stories and the aunts told stories. William told us about when Mama was little, like Jack. Papa told stories about Grandfather trying to train his first horse, the horse pulling him through the barn and out to the slough.

Everyone laughed, and it was almost

like the laughter floated out over the prairie, pulled by the winds, here and there and back again.

The sounds of voices and laughter are like little pebbles
    All around us.
    We can reach up and scoop them up in our hands
    Holding them close to us.
    Saving them forever.

When I read my journal to Grandfather, he smiled.

"Forever," he said, more to himself than to me.

He walked over to the driveway and

bent down. Then he came back to where I stood. He took my hand and put a pebble there.

"I . . . ," he said.

"Love . . ." He put another pebble there.

"You," he said as he placed the last one.

I stared at them for a long time, then closed my hand over them. When I looked up again, Grandfather was gone.

10

The next day Aunt Lou was the very first up in the morning again.

"I've driven a car," she said to Papa. "Now it is time to ride a horse. Only five more days before we have to go back East. It's time."

"'Old lady on a dapple . . .'" began Jack before Mama put her hand over his mouth.

Grandfather and Papa smiled.

"Zeke, maybe," said Aunt Lou.

Papa looked at Mama.

"I remember a long time ago," he said softly. "Do you?"

Mama nodded.

"When I first came here I wanted to learn to ride your wildest horse, Jack, and to fix the roof . . ."

"And to plow and almost everything

else," said Papa.

"And she did," said Caleb with a smile. "She wore overalls, too."

"I had a lot to learn," said Mama.

"Well, Sarah taught *me* how to swim when she first came here," said Caleb.

"In the slough?" exclaimed Aunt Harriet.

"You bet," said Caleb.

"You bet," echoed Jack, making everyone laugh.

"I remember skinny-dipping in Maine," Caleb said. "That water was cold."

"I'll ride Zeke," said Aunt Lou, starting to walk to the barn.

"No," said Papa, going after her and taking her hand. "I'll saddle up Molly."

"I'll go with you," said Grandfather. "This time we'll take a quiet and slow ride around the slough. If that's possible for you," he called after Aunt Lou.

"Boppa," said Jack to Grandfather. He held out his arms.

"All right, all right. A short ride," said Grandfather.

Grandfather, Papa, and Aunt Lou went to the paddock to bring in the horses. Jack followed Grandfather, walking just behind him, his arms behind his back like Grandfather's.

"Little Boppa and big Boppa," said Caleb, making Mama laugh.

We watched them call in the horses and saddle up, Papa lifting Jack up to ride with Grandfather. Aunt Mattie had gotten out a set of paints and a small easel. She began to paint the prairie, the browns and greens of the land, with spots of wildflowers, the blue of the huge sky.

Aunt Lou and Grandfather and Jack slowly rode out through the meadow. Birds flew up from the grasses where they rode, redwings and meadowlarks. A vulture wheeled high against the clouds. I watched Grandfather, tall and straight, Jack in front of him, pointing at something somewhere on the prairie.

"I hope you paint that," I said to Aunt Mattie.

Aunt Mattie smiled at me.

"You don't need a painting," she said. "If you close your eyes you'll see that scene forever."

I closed my eyes and waited. Aunt Mattie was right.

I could see it.

It is nighttime. We sit under the tents, still there from the wedding.

The aunts and William drink coffee by candlelight.

"Sing, Boppa," says Jack.

There is a silence.

"Please," says Jack.

Grandfather begins to sing "Billy Boy."

"Oh, where have you been, Billy Boy,
    Billy Boy.
Oh, where have you been, charming
    Billy?

I have been to seek a wife
She's the joy of my life.
But she's a young thing and cannot leave
   her mother."

Then Aunt Mattie sings, too, and
Jack's small voice sings the "billy boys."

"Can she bake a cherry pie, Billy Boy,
   Billy Boy?
Can she bake a cherry pie, charming
   Billy?
She can bake a cherry pie, quick's a cat
   can blink its eye.
But she's a young thing and cannot leave
   her mother."

Jack leans back on Grandfather's
shoulder. Aunt Mattie's knitting needles
click in the dark. The moon rises. The can-
dle flickers in the gentle prairie wind.
   I close my eyes to keep everything there.

11

The photographer Joshua came to take a family picture. He waited for the aunts to comb their hair and put red on their cheeks. He grinned at Mama.

"I remember years ago when you first came here. I took a picture of you and Jacob and Caleb—he was little then. And Anna. And the dogs." He looked at Lottie and Nick.

"They're a little older now."

"We all are," said Mama. "Anna married Justin this past week."

"So I heard," said Joshua.

Joshua shook Grandfather's hand.

"Hello, John," he said.

"I'm older, too," said Grandfather with a smile.

The aunts came out onto the porch. Aunt Harriet and Aunt Mattie wore their traveling dresses and fancy shoes. Aunt Lou wore her overalls.

"I want to be remembered in my overalls," said Aunt Lou.

"You will," said Grandfather. "Believe me, you will."

Mama and William laughed.

"That's how *we* think of you," said William.

"You see me every day," Aunt Lou said to William. "You don't have to remember me. But I probably won't get back here anytime soon."

Suddenly my chest felt tight.

"You could stay longer," I said.

"Oh, Cassie," said Aunt Harriet. "We have gardens to get back to. Things to take care of. Meg has been taking care of Lou's dog."

My eyes filled up with tears.

"Cassie, dear . . . ," said Aunt Mattie,

putting her arms around me. "We'd love to stay. We'll come back again."

This made me cry harder.

"Cassie, next year you can come visit us in Maine," said William. "Would you like that?"

I nodded.

"But that's next year," I said sadly.

"I'm ready!" called Joshua. "Gather up, everyone. Wipe those tears away, Cassie."

The aunts arranged themselves next to Mama and Papa. William patted the dogs. Grandfather stood next to me, Jack in his arms.

"Wait," said Papa. "Someone's coming."

Dust rose as a car drove up the road. Mama shaded her eyes from the sun. Joshua turned to watch.

"It's Anna and Justin!" I said.

"We couldn't miss the family picture," Anna called out the car window.

"My first," said Justin.

"Not your last," said Grandfather. "You can stand behind Cassie."

Anna smoothed my hair back. Justin poked me.

"All looking here now," called Joshua.

"You're not much to look at," said Grandfather softly. "I'd rather look at Zeke in the meadow."

"Zeke in the meadow," said Jack.

We laughed, and just as I looked up at Grandfather, Joshua took a picture. Joshua took many more as the aunts laughed and the sun rose high in the sky. A wind came up and Aunt Harriet's hat flew away. Papa ran and brought it back to her. And soon, Jack fell asleep. Grandfather handed him to Mama and put his arm around me.

Far off, the cattle moved to the slough for water. Zeke ran with Molly along the fence. Lottie and Nick stood between Grandfather and me, their fur warm.

"Beautiful," said Joshua.

"Yes," said Grandfather, looking out at the prairie.

"Oh, yes," said Aunt Harriet.

"Oh, yes," said Jack, half awake, half asleep.

Yes.

———•———

Joshua began packing up. Grandfather walked to the barn, Jack following him. Joshua turned.

"John! Stop for a moment. I want to take a picture of you in front of the barn. Where's your hat?"

"Here," I said.

I ran over and handed Grandfather his big black hat. Jack reached up and took his hand.

"Cassie," said Grandfather. "I want you in this picture."

Joshua nodded at me.

"Go on," he said.

I took Grandfather's other hand. Little swirls of wind made circles in the dirt in the yard. I could smell the roses on the fence.

"Smile," called Joshua.

"You don't have to smile if you don't want to," said Grandfather.

I grinned.

The camera shutter clicked.

"That's it," called Joshua. "The end."

Later, all of my life, I would hear the echo of Joshua's words.

All of my life.

The end.

12

After Joshua left, it was quiet. Grandfather and Jack went to make sure the animals had water. The rest of us sat under the tents.

"We'll have to take these down soon," said Papa.

"I suppose," said Mama. "Maybe we can leave them up for a while."

Papa smiled at her.

"Maybe."

"Maybe you can leave them up until Cassie gets married," said Anna.

"I already had my wedding," I said.

"That's right," said Justin. "You had a grand wedding. Where's that groom?"

"He's in the barn with Grandfather and Jack," I said.

As if he had heard me, Nick began barking in the barn. Papa stood up.

"What's that about? Nick doesn't bark all that often," he said.

Jack came to the door of the barn and looked at us. He was not smiling. His small voice carried on the summer wind.

"Boppa?"

Mama stood up. Papa began to run to the barn.

"Cassie!" he called to me. "Come get Jack."

For some reason, I couldn't move. William touched me on the shoulder and ran to Jack.

"Boppa!" said Jack more loudly when William picked him up. He pointed over William's shoulder back at the barn.

"Sarah?" Papa's voice sounded weak. His face was pale.

"Sarah. I need your help. Now."

I started to go with Mama, but Aunt Lou held me.

"I want to be with Grandfather," I said.

"I know," she said, putting her arms around me.

I began to cry. My heart hurt.

I knew. Somehow, I knew.

My grandfather died in the barn where I had found him when I was a little girl. He had come back then to see the place he loved. He had come back to see Papa. Today he lay down in the hay and closed his eyes there.

Papa let me see him for a minute because I wanted to. For a minute Grandfather looked just the same. I thought maybe he would open his eyes and smile at me. But he didn't. And that made him look different.

When I looked up at Papa he was crying, tears coming down his face like rain.

That made me frightened.

"Papa?"

"It's all right, Cassie. It's all right to be sad."

I reached over and took his hand and stood there until Mama came to get me.

Jack was very quiet. He wouldn't sit on anyone's lap. He wouldn't smile.

Just before they came to take Grandfather away I took Jack for a long walk so he wouldn't have to see.

"You don't have to do that, Cassie," Mama said.

"I know. I want to."

Jack and I walked up to the hilltop behind the house and sat under the one tree that grew there. Jack didn't look at me. He picked a piece of grass and stared at it.

The aunts had told me that Jack didn't

understand. But I knew better. I took a deep breath.

"Jack?"

Jack didn't look up.

"Jack, I want you to listen. I want you to listen to something very important."

There was silence. Insects buzzed in the grass. Finally Jack looked up at me. His eyes were blue and sharp.

"Grandfather loved you, Jack. He loved you more than anyone else."

Jack stared at me. After a long time he reached over and touched me.

Tears came to my eyes. I smiled because I knew what he meant.

"Yes, he loved me, too. And we don't ever have to forget him. We won't."

Jack didn't say anything, but I knew he understood my words. We sat for a long, long time. The sun began to set. I stood up. Nothing seemed the same. The land didn't look the same anymore. The sky looked different. I stared down at the farm that was once Grandfather's farm.

There was a small rustle beside me. Jack took my hand, his hand warm in mine. Together we walked down the hill.

———•◆•———

Grandfather would have liked his funeral. The aunts dressed up like they had for the wedding. Even Aunt Lou wore a dress and high-heeled shoes. All the towns-people came. They told stories about Grandfather. Sometimes they had conver-sations about him.

"Once he saved a horse of mine."

"That horse never should have been saved!"

"I remember how he loved to cut the hay."

"He hated cutting the hay."

"Oh, no he didn't. Sometimes he sang when he cut the hay."

"He taught me how to ride a horse," said Aunt Lou. "And he was nice about it."

"He didn't love my music," said Aunt Harriet.

"He did, in the end," said Aunt Mattie.

Caleb told about when Grandfather first came.

"Cassie found him. He had been gone for many years, and Cassie talked to him so much, as if she wanted to fill up all those years. He couldn't make her stop, but he never cared. Because he loved her."

"Cassie?" said Papa.

"Grandfather gave me a wedding," I said. No one laughed when I said it.

Words about Grandfather floated around our heads. And then, when it was time to bury him, it was quiet again.

Papa's voice was clear and strong and sad.

"We were stronger having him," he said.

Tears came to Papa's eyes, and Mama put her arm around him. And then Jack walked up to Papa and then away a bit. As everyone watched, he did a little dance, turning around and around with his hands up in the air just the way Grandfather had done. Grandfather's dance.

"He understands," said Mama, starting to cry. "Jack *understands.*"

Jack did the dance again. Then, for the first time in a long time, Jack smiled.

It is quiet here without Caleb and William and the aunts. Mostly quiet without Grandfather. There is a great space where he used to be.

Jack is quiet some of the time. Other times he acts as if Grandfather might be just around the corner. Or in the barn. Sometimes he wears Grandfather's big black hat, so he acts like him and looks like him, too.

Joshua came and brought us the family pictures. And there we are, Aunt Harriet with her hat flying away in the wind, me looking up and smiling at Grandfather, Jack asleep on Mama's lap. Lottie and Nick leaning next to us.

And there is the picture of Grandfather in front of the barn with his big black hat: me on one side, Jack on the other, standing so like Grandfather.

When Jack saw the picture he went to get Grandfather's black hat. He put it on. He pointed to the picture.

"Boppa," he whispered.

Grandfather is here.

Author's Note

I began writing about the Witting family
in *Sarah, Plain and Tall* and have been telling
their stories ever since. It is bittersweet for
me to end my writing relationship with
them and all the extended family in the
book *Grandfather's Dance*. I know I won't end
my *personal* relationship with them; the
characters are too much a part of my life.
Their landscape is mine, one I left behind
many years ago—partly my father's landscape in North Dakota, my mother's in
Kansas, and mine in Wyoming. I live in the
East now, but writing these stories has kept
my childhood close.

The "real" Sarah was my step-great-
great-grandmother, though I never knew

many things about her. For my books, I invented her personality, the family and life she left in Maine, and her thoughts and fears. In many ways, this has strengthened my connection with my past.

The dogs and cats are friends to me; some I have patterned after my own pets, past and present. And the grandfather is modeled after my own father, who told stories about the prairie, the horses, the farm dogs, the storms, the harsh winters, and the droughts. Somehow, he is there in every story.

And so am I.

Read all the books about the Witting family by Newbery Medalist Patricia MacLachlan

Sarah, Plain and Tall
Winner of the Newbery Medal
When Papa puts an ad in the paper asking for a wife, he receives a letter from Sarah Elisabeth Wheaton. Anna and Caleb wait and wonder. Will Sarah be nice? Will she like them?

Skylark
When a drought sweeps across the prairie, Sarah takes Anna and Caleb back east, where they will be safe. Anna is homesick and she misses Papa. Will they ever be a family again?

Caleb's Story
When Caleb sets out to write the family story, he fears there will be nothing to write about—until Cassie discovers a mysterious old man in the barn, and everything changes.

More Perfect than the Moon
Cassie doesn't know how she feels about change. But change is inevitable, even on the prairie. And Cassie learns that unexpected surprises can bring great joy.

Grandfather's Dance
Nothing could be more perfect than Cassie's entire family coming together for her sister Anna's wedding. But as Cassie learns, sometimes the hardest part about loving someone is having to say good-bye.

www.harpercollinschildrens.com

Joanna Cotler Books
An Imprint of HarperCollinsPublishers

HarperTrophy®
An Imprint of HarperCollinsPublishers